TEENY WITCH
and
Christmas MAGIC

by LIZ MATTHEWS
illustrated by CAROLYN LOH

Troll Associates

It was the most exciting night of the year.
It was Christmas Eve. Teeny Witch was busy
in her room. She was wrapping gifts for her
three aunts.

"Aunt Icky will love this wooden spoon," said Teeny Witch. "It has an extra long handle. She can use it to stir the smelly brews she likes to make."

Teeny Witch giggled as she wrapped Aunt Ticky's present. It was a cuckoo clock. Her Aunt Ticky liked weird and wacky things.

5

Aunt Vicky's gift was the best of all.

"This will be a perfect addition to Aunt Vicky's ugly bug collection," said Teeny. Teeny had bought her Aunt Vicky an ant farm.

"At last, my presents are all wrapped," said Teeny. "Now it is time to hang my stocking."

Teeny Witch tried to stay cheerful as she walked through the big, old house. It wasn't easy. There were no Christmas lights. There were no Christmas decorations. And in the living room there was no Christmas tree.

Teeny's aunts were a bit strange. They liked Christmas and Christmas presents. But they didn't like bright decorations or cheerful Christmas trees. They liked their house to look dark and spooky.

Teeny found her aunts standing by the window.
"Look at it snow," said Aunt Icky.
"It's so pretty," said Aunt Ticky.
"YUCK!" groaned Aunt Vicky. "I like mud better."

"I'm going to hang my stocking now," said Teeny.

"Be careful where you hammer," said Aunt Vicky.

"Don't hammer near the loose stone in the fireplace," said Aunt Icky. "It may fall out."

Tap! Tap! Tap! Teeny tacked up her stocking.
"There," she said. "I'm all finished."
"Very good," said Aunt Icky. "Now it is time for bed.
It is late and Santa is on his way."

Teeny's three aunts put her to bed.
They tucked Teeny in and kissed her good
night. Then they went to bed, too. Soon
everyone was fast asleep.

Teeny was dreaming about Santa Claus when a strange sound woke her up.

Plunk! Clunk!

"Ouch!" someone yelled.

Teeny Witch jumped out of bed. She went into the living room to see what was going on.

Teeny Witch peeked around a corner. She saw an amazing sight! Sitting on the floor in front of the fireplace was Santa! He was rubbing his head and moaning. Near his bag of gifts was the loose stone from the fireplace.

"Oh, my goodness!" said Teeny Witch. "The stone must have fallen out and hit Santa on the head. Santa! Santa!" she cried. "Are you all right?"

"I-I think I'm o-o-okay," Santa said. Santa tried to get up. But his legs wobbled. He could barely stand. Santa was so dizzy, Teeny Witch had to help him into a chair. "You need to rest awhile," Teeny said.

"I can't," Santa answered. "I have three more houses to go to before going to the next town. If I stop here I'll be late. And then some boy or girl may not have a merry Christmas."

Teeny Witch thought for a minute. Suddenly an idea
popped into her head.

"I can deliver those presents for you while you rest,"
Teeny suggested. "When I come back you will feel better."

"Thank you, but no," said Santa. "I have to go."
Again he tried to stand. The room seemed to spin
around and around. Poor Santa had to sit down.

"Okay, Teeny Witch," said Santa. "Tonight you will be my special helper. My reindeer know where to go. And my list is in my bag."

"GREAT!" shouted Teeny Witch.

"Put on my hat," Santa said to Teeny when she was ready to go. "Its special Christmas magic will help you."

Teeny slipped Santa's furry red cap onto her head. It gave her a happy tingling feeling from her nose down to her toes. Teeny picked up Santa's bag. Thanks to the magic cap, it didn't even feel heavy.

"Be careful," Santa said as he sipped the milk Teeny had left for him.

"I will," Teeny promised.

And, in a flash, she was on the snowy roof.
Santa's sleigh and reindeer were before her.
Teeny climbed into the sleigh.

"Santa is resting. And he made me his special helper," Teeny said.

The reindeer nodded as if they understood.

Teeny tugged on the reins. Jingle! Jingle! Jingle! went the bells. Up into the air the sleigh and reindeer flew.

"Wow," said Teeny as she soared over rooftops. "This is fun!"

The Gomez family was first on the list. Their house was easy to find. It had lots of bright, twinkling lights all around. The sleigh landed on the roof. Teeny hopped out with the big bag of toys.

Down the chimney slid Santa's helper. Quickly, Teeny Witch filled all of the stockings hanging from the mantel. Then, lickety-split, back up the chimney she zipped.

"HO! HO! HO! LET'S GO!"
Teeny Witch shouted to the
reindeer. "Jimmy and Judy's
house is next."

Jingle! Jingle! Jingle!
The sleigh sped through the
falling snow to the next stop.

Teeny went right to work. She checked Santa's list
once and then she checked it twice just to be sure.
Jimmy got drums and a train set. Judy got a toy piano
and a big talking doll.

Before long, Teeny was on her way to the last house.
It was Joey Jones' home.

"Oh, how pretty," Teeny said
when she saw the Jones' tree.
It was cheerful and bright and
on the tippy-top there was a big,
golden star.

Teeny arranged the toys under the beautiful Christmas tree. "I wish we could have a tree like this," Teeny said. "And I wish our house had lights and decorations, too." But Teeny Witch knew her Christmas wish could never come true.

Soon it was time to go.

She climbed into the sleigh. "Back to my house, please," she called.

Away flew the reindeer.
"My house is just ahead,"
Teeny told the reindeer.
   But the house she saw didn't
look anything like her spooky
old house.

Santa's sleigh landed on Teeny's roof. Teeny Witch
slid down the chimney. The room she found at the
bottom was a delight to behold.

There were garlands hanging from the walls.

Decorations were everywhere. Best of all, in the middle of the room was a Christmas tree full of lights and shiny ornaments.

"Merry Christmas, Teeny Witch!" Santa called.

Teeny Witch was so surprised. "How did this happen?" she asked.

"It was Santa," Aunt Icky explained.

"Santa?" Teeny didn't understand. "But he was so dizzy when I left."

"One of my headache brews cured that," said Aunt Icky.

"And then Santa showed us where to get decorations and a tree," Aunt Ticky added.

"But you don't like decorations or Christmas trees," Teeny Witch said.

"Santa changed our minds," Aunt Vicky said.
"He said even a spooky old house should look special
on Christmas. And he is right."

"I think the house looks kind of nice this
way," Aunt Icky said.

Teeny Witch smiled from ear to ear. "This
really is a special Christmas," she said.

Teeny Witch took off Santa's cap. "But how did you know about my wish?" she whispered to Santa.

Santa pointed at his hat. "There really is magic in that cap," he laughed.

Santa put the hat on his head. He filled Teeny's stocking with toys. "Ho! Ho! Ho!" he chuckled. Santa winked at Teeny and her three aunts. Then, whoosh! Up the chimney he flew!

From the window, Teeny Witch and her three aunts watched Santa's sleigh streak through the sky.

"Goodbye!" called Teeny Witch. "Thank you for making this Christmas so special."

Then Teeny Witch went to bed and fell fast asleep.

And when she woke up, it was Christmas morning!